The Rose Covered Cottage

by Douglas C. Granum

Chapter 1
The Year 1917, War

Surely, we knew it couldn't last, but hoped, oh my God, yes! We talked of love forever. How long is that? A lifetime, a year, a month, a day, an hour, a moment, a kiss?

You see, I believed it. All of it. I willed myself, until that photograph.

How silly I was, love doesn't last forever, even if it is chiseled in stone. Water, winds, sands, shadows, the weather, all erode it, like a diorama it becomes a blank, staring thing. Am I being too harsh, this seamless hope of love?

You, you return to your tattooed French princess, me to my scullery tasks, my glass slippers cast aside like frail crystal poems on the forest's ferny floor. Me? From a distance I dance, twist in pain as the drying process begins. I am keening, cursing little woman crawling in the face of despair. What was, will it never be again?

We kissed, oh those first tender, exploring kisses. We delicately, ever so gently, touched each other, consoled one another, reassured each other. Yes, touch me, it's ok. You softly murmured sweet little words. We breathed warmly into each others ears, following with our tongues, so tickling, so thrilling.

We felt with our hands. This is how we met. No one had ever unbuttoned my

blouse before. I'd never pulled my sweater over my head, saying you will love my
breasts. You, flicking my eager nipples
with your tongue. Sinking in delight, in the
spring time. Passion.

The wind-driven blue-patterned quilt
of sky, the great sapphire dome sailed above
us when the orchard was in blossom. Our
orchard, the winds scattering apple blossoms in the field grass.

The beach steaming at low tide, nour-
ishing spring sun. We did love each other
then, didn't we? You did love me didn't
you?

Even before I met you that day while
walking on the beach, I was weeding the
garden, planting drifts of purple fragrant violets, cutting driftwood for the steam bath,
and then there you were. I was so lonely
then until I met you. Before I met you I was
independent, now, mush.

But why ask? For your lips were there,

miraculously I found them.

What have you done to me? Spring love, young love, so stimulating, so devastating.

Well you have kissed me now, yet it still rains in the chambers of my heart. How many kinds of rain?

Since your last frigid note I wander the woodlands, calling your name into the night. Owls, small little furry creatures, hear me. The whole forest of creatures hear my plea for help. Singing frogs listen to my impassioned voice, abruptly stopping their song. All is quiet, then slowly they begin to sing again. First one makes a tentative rasping, clicking sound, then two others. Then one from clear over on the other side of the pond, our pond, then soon a forest opera, and all join in.

Their song of joy and nature brings me tears once more. I think of you, wondering what does one fill lost love with? It hurts when I think it can't possibly hurt more. I hear the evening robin's aria, it's solo operatic voice, it's descending crescendo, and my heart is broken once again.

Love is not seamless, lost love is blades of glass. Color them discordant. One day will I look back and see all along that I was dying?

"Give it up," I said to myself, yet a rooster crows, waves on the beach murmur words to me, your words, your voice. Then, just as I see you hold out your hand to me, you disappear. In the darkness you laugh, I can hear you, but can't see you. Are you there?

"I am over here," says your voice on the beach. I run to the sound, you are not there. "Here I am," you cry. I run there, you are not there either, you have moved once more. I wake up feeling another sharp wound. Hal, hope gave me the courage to withstand your abuse.

A seal breaks water on calm nights out

in the cove, breathing out, sometimes it coughs.

It is so close, I feel as I am awakened from my restless sleep, I wonder that it is perhaps you, standing beside our bed in the loft. That last thought is twisted, I know, but then love and pain destroy one's ability to think clearly. I think to myself that must be love as I listen for your voice. Do you still love me? Do you even remember me?

I know this is not rational. You are far away, yet maybe you have come home and have not told me, perhaps to surprise me. Oh, that would be so wonderful Hal.

You will think that I am mad. Perhaps I am, mad with longing, mad with desire. Maybe at the bottom of my sharp edged shards of love I am just deranged, with the rampaging emotions stampeding, trampling what is left of my straining, yearning soul.

Love lies, desiccated, in the bottom of

my febrile skull, like a dead rat. I held your .357 Smith and Wesson the other night, with the pearl handles, the cold blue steel. I seem to remember you telling me Grandpa Jack carried this pistol in the first Great War in France. I was digging in your drawer upstairs and there it lay, like a blued black widow, ominous.

What of our future in this dream I call life? Will it be that someday I will see that I am staring at nothing from something that was?

Sometimes, like last night, it was gloomy. I could die, but not if you love me and are coming home; I couldn't die then. I think too much, I know, but then before you I feel nothing existed. After you will anything exist?

People die without a vision of the future, something to pull them along. I see no future lying here tonight, and nothing is pulling me along.

This then, perhaps someday we will be photos in an old barn, or in a photograph like the one in our wedding picture. They will notice the pretty silver frame, like the one on the mantel over the fireplace. Maybe in that antique shop, or they will be exploring in a garage sale. They will see us, barely glancing at us, instead looking at the silver frame. Is it possible when looking at the photograph of us, you and me Hal, looking with loving beauty into each other's eyes from another time and place, they will only see the frame.

There will be fresh plum blossoms, cherries, jasmine, peach blossoms. Remember the photograph Aunt Cora took of us with the farm in the background? Will they see our love, or, more likely, will they rip us from the frame for the frame alone, and as we twist and spin to the dusty floor, blankly staring from that oh so gorgeous day, will they turn and not notice our young thrill of love? "How much is the frame?" they will ask, stepping on us, lying on the floor, as they walk out.

There is the war, we are in love, aren't we? Aren't you? I am. What is this thing called love? A place where someone does more than say "I love you." A place where you are touched, caressed, a place where there is nothing else but us?

But now you are gone, the war, the distance, did you really love me as you said? I try to be strong, to understand your letter, but then love changes everything and I am changed. When you said good-bye, I died a little and each day since.

Who is the girl in the photo on the Eiffel Tower? Did you really mean what you said, or are you a long way from me and our home? The distance, the war, the machine gun cropping death machine always present, it is always present, isn't it? I am sorry to ask, but it is raining so hard tonight, the far shore of the cove is a grey smear.

I feel naked, alone, maybe like one of those white grubs, that twists and turns when we uncover it under the bark of rotted logs.

Did I ever really understand what I said, what you said?

How silly I am. Are you in the arms of another now? So now I write to you, but no matter what I write, or what you write, the pen on the page can never be your lips, the round strokes of your words can never be your arms. I need you.

I dreamed last night of some kind of gray ship painted with golden angels. War was exploding smoke, and daylight was changing rapidly from daylight to dark and back, again and again, all in black and white.

Once more I saw us in the photograph from that bird song spring of fragrance, and now in this vivid nightmare.

Why do we call them nightmares? I don't know, but there we lay, torn and walked on, our love trampled. Is our love trampled? Hal, have you crushed our love?

We were so lovely in our time. What now, you and me, my love?

I awoke, drinking water from your special etched red glass, falling back to sleep listening to the rain falling from the eaves of our cottage. Is it still our cottage?

As I drifted back into that nightmarish grey dream once again, you and I lay in that yellowing photograph on the floor. Time is lethal.

I noticed something I had not seen before. In the background was our new barn, made from those long cedar boards you split from our own forest. Is it still our own forest? Over your manly shoulders were the reins for the horses, what now?

We are still together, if only in this dream, or is it more, does love last? I dreamed I was sweetly, gently kissing your eyes, that I could taste the salt from your lips, and awoke to find it was only my own tears. Is this it then, that this desire, hope, caring, is this it, that we are passionately part of something else, and we hope it is part of us?

For the most part, that is so, but when we are in love, love is fresh, excitingly vital, what else is there to think of but the thrill of love everlasting, love forever?

However good that may sound, it isn't always the case, it is also often a lie. We belong to the power we choose to obey. I choose you Hal, do you choose me?

A simple question, but I hang on a thread here.

I went to the little county museum the other day, looking, as I always do, at people's faces, especially their eyes. When I walked out on the street, looking at the people walking along, I saw the same time-distant eyes that were on the photographs and paintings from years and years ago. Are we that, man, woman, the small world, are we all one, or do we even exist in this chimera?

Is it possible that you exist, you, Harold, on paintings from a hundred years ago? It is this for me, I need your warmth, your heat, your eyes, your hands. Do you, for me, exist at all? Oh, God, Harold, I am cold and afraid; bring me your heat.

"The grave's a fine and private place, but none, I think, do there embrace."

I lay in the loft this morning, thinking of you, of course, only you, in your fox hole, you with exploding shells over head, you with others close by wanting to kill you. I wondered what do you think of. Do you think of me?

But why would you think of me with bullets singing songs of dying over your head? Life is so dear. I am here, you are there.

You know that I am lonely, only lonely for you, Harold. When we are lonely, we say, do little things that really don't make much sense. Maybe that is what these musings are about, senseless longing with the realization that you may never, I tremble at the thought, that you may never come back to me.

Take your love out of me and what's left is an empty shell, dead beach drift carried by the tide up and back until it is dust.

I have blown out the candle, and I wanted to tell you I sleep on your side of the bed now, by the window. Tonight, I have pulled the doona around me for comfort. With the storm blasting through the trees I, as usual, close my eyes, thinking back to those times when your love and arms held me, lost and discovered.

Chapter 2
The year 1980

I am looking at Juliet. She has just stepped out of her scented bath. She has wrapped a soft pink french towel around her waist, her breasts, steaming ever so slightly, are exposed, desirous. Her rich tan nipples, soft, relaxed, magenta rouge, framboise. As she looks at herself in the mirror, running her hands through her red hair, her eyes find mine.

I am standing close behind her. I am also nude, though no towel. I have just stepped out of our heated, steaming shower. As she coyly watches me, I close my shower-warm hands over her moist, sweet, milk colored breasts, then lightly, ever so lightly, touch her, skipping my hands down the summer landscape of her rolling velvet belly. She trembles involuntarily, shuttering, shaking slightly, as my hands pass further into the cloud like red feathers of her thighs. My hands rest there, I can see them, they look strong, interesting in the mirror. As I look over her nude shoulders, I look at myself looking back. I like the look of my eyes. I like Juliet's eyes. She lifts them without raising her head, looking into the mirror back at me. I push lightly with my hands. Juliet smiles at me. I see myself over her warm shoulders in the mirror. I murmur into her neck, lightly touching my lips on her exposed neck, I feel aroused, skin to skin, no lace.

The rich, damp fragrances rising around her are making me lightheaded. Her perfume Caleche, with its smells of citrus and a rose floral heart. I bought this for her in Paris. It mixes, spring like, in and around her freshness.

There is in between our warm, nude bodies a definite mingling of opulence, sweet as the honied fragrance of an old-fashioned garden rose. This scent is calling to me, its siren call is of her sex, with a shouting bottom note of desire.

She slowly rotates in my arms, grazing her erect nipples across my chest, as she faces me. Then, fastening her arms around my neck, while closing her eyes, she kisses me deeply; tongue.

Her fragrance is all floral, while hidden somewhere in this tangled bouquet of fragrance is one of simple purity and garden rose. Looking at us in the mirror, smelling summer rose, I remember that late summer afternoon when we, Juliet, Annette, Hans, and I, broke into the rose covered cottage at the end of French's Bay.

It was one of those remarkable, unique days where green magic rises on each trembling blade of grass. Over every flower an angel, filled with the sweetness of life, softly, breathily said, "Grow."

A most sumptuous, self-indulgent day we spent there, while that night phosphorescence lit the shapes of our nude, starlit bodies as we swam in a small cove full of late summer moonlight. Fish, small streaking rockets of blue green light, shot along the bottom of the cove into darker shadowed waters at our approach. We were all in love. We were in love with each other, in love with the sky, the sea, the forest, in love with love.

It was early afternoon, we were all excited with the thought of lunching on the grass. Remember Edouard Manet's painting, Le Déjeuner sur l'herbe? That was our goal.

I didn't plan what happened; none of us planned what happened. All of us remember the day with pain, yet pleasure. With wild honey often comes the sting.

Our day started innocently enough. We agreed that we would picnic somewhere in the country, that we would find a place secluded, away from the highways. A place where we could relax. A place where we could put out a blanket, maybe write poetry. Hans brought his guitar, perhaps a love song, "Misty," walk in the woods, have a day to ourselves. A place where we could walk the beach, swim in the nude, and perhaps mimic Edouard Manet's famous painting, Le Déjeuner sur l'herbe, "Luncheon on the Grass."

We drove south toward French's Bay in

separate cars, probing logging roads along the way, finding most with cables across them, steel gates. There were signs by large logging companies, threatening mayhem and lawsuits if we so much as set foot on their privately owned land.

The area around French's Bay was new territory for us. Sometimes the rough roads ended in logged clearings, certainly no place to lay out blankets in dried bulldozer tracks, no swimming. Some roads ended in people's yards, where large dogs barked at us, chasing us alongside the car until we got back on the pavement.

Suddenly, while aimlessly driving along, on one winding, poor gravel road we found a partly overgrown old driveway.

Hans and Annette drove right past it. We stopped, honked at them to turn around.

At first it didn't look like a road, but then we saw the sign. It had been cut out of a cedar board, but it was now too old to read forever. As we stopped, we still tried to read it, but could only make out two letters, a capitol "S" and an "R". The rest was covered in moss, or had been eroded by decades of runneling rain.

The overgrown drive had thick grass and a heavy cover of moss. Small, thin alder saplings grew thickly beneath dark, dripping, virgin cedars and firs. The sun slanted down through drops of rain water, on the tips of each branch from the morning rains, like crystal Christmas ornaments.

As I gazed far down the old drive, I could make out what looked like a sunny clearing in the deep forest ahead.

Hans drove his old Volvo off the road, pushing between the salmon berry and huckleberry bushes, scraping the sides of his car. The thorn covered salmon berry bushes, the green alder saplings, all were scraping his car as he finally forced his way into a meadow surrounded by moss-covered cedar split rail fences. The meadow sloped down to a quiet, saltwater cove.

We didn't see the cabin.

As Hans stopped his old Volvo in the center of the meadow, we pulled along side. Annette, who was wearing a white Turkish coat with a beret, jumped out of the car and ran for the beach, with Hans running behind her, trying to snatch her beret off her head. As she ran, she pulled her arms from the coat and let it drop. Hans tripped on the coat, falling, yelling, laughing all at the same time. Annette stopped, ran back, and fell on Hans, kissing him on his knee where his pants were torn. They sat for a moment, then stood up, holding hands, quietly hugging, holding each other as they walked the rest of the way to the pebbled beach. Hans had blood on his knee, and Annette had blood on her lips.

Stepping out of the car, Juliet called urgently to me to come look. "Look, look,

look," she gestured with her arms out while spinning around and around. The rich meadow grass was tossed with red rose pedals everywhere, while in the air courting hummingbirds were flying in looping, high-speed dives, then arcing back up into the sky to dive once more, again and again. At the bottom of each dive they made a little chit chit chit zzzzzzeeeee.

The top of each fence post was covered in a gauze of vibrant jade green moss, as were the old cedar rails. Each rail was wrapped in jade gauze.

At the upper end of the field, surrounded by the jade green fences, stood a very old, embattled, staggering barn. The old barn was surrounded by forest, dark and near.

Embattled because nature was advancing each moment of each day and winning the battle. On nature's side, there was time, rot, wind, rain, mold, rats, termites, and that other curse of old buildings, gravity. On the barn's side of this tangle with eternity, this unequal battle, not much, completely one sided.

As someone once said, "An ugly building can make a beautiful ruin." In this case the barn had been beautiful in its youth. It was still beautiful, though ravaged. Like a once beautiful opera diva, no amount of powder or lipstick will ever fill the wrinkles and the gnawing, gnashing destruction of time.

This graceful, old, beautiful barn appeared to have been built of hand-split timbers. I could see, even from a distance, that the hand-split shingles from virgin timber were thick cedar. The side boards of the barn were twenty inches wide, maybe thirty feet long, standing vertically.

Sensual magic hung in the heavy, gateau like air. The barn undulated over the ground, leaning, sagging, matching the roll of the land it was built on. The forest smelled of resin and maple.

Walking to the beach, we watched as Annette and Hans stripped off their jeans down to their underwear. They then walked out into the quiet, gray green waters of the cove. Ducks quietly swam further out into the cove, looking over their iridescent green backs, as Annette and Hans waded into the water. The ducks left small, sunlit V-shaped wakes on the calm water. Further out in the cove, a large log, loosened from the shore by the rising tide, carried a cormorant with its wings out drying.

We found the beach was covered in small, dark, flat pebbles with bits of white shell. On the mirrored surface of the cove, leaves, seaweed, and rose petals all drifted on the rising tide. Juliet took off her skirt as I peeled off my pants to my black silk underwear. We waded out, our feet pink on the small, smooth, dark pebbles. Small frothy bubbles formed between my warm toes.

The cold salt water closing around our ankles was icy, shocking. I felt water rise to the backs of my knees as Juliet waded after a rose pedal floating near by. Her legs were covered with goose bumps.

Standing in the cold water I could see small crabs moving beneath the water on the dark bottom of the cove. Little wisps of nori green seaweed were drifting midwater, beneath the surface on the incoming tide.

As I looked over at Annette, I could see her nipples erect beneath her purple high-necked satin chemise. As the waters rose, soaking my underwear, Annette's pink flowered silk panties were also covering with chilled seawater. I could see through the wet silk the dark red of her pubic hair quivering beneath the icy water.

At that moment Juliet stepped on a small flounder camouflaged in the sandy gravels on the black bottom of the cove. Her startled scream echoed off the trees and around the cove. The heron and a few of the ducks flew up.

I reached out, grabbing her to keep her from falling. She half swam, half walked into my arms, where I held her close, laughing while kissing her salt washed face. In that second, I tasted the different salt of the sea and her frightened, happy tears. From her mouth, there always was the scent of passion. She always wanted me, I always wanted her.

She pulled me deeper into the cold, late summer water as her hands were seeking inside my soaked black silk underwear. I felt strong, she made me feel that way, all muscle, a king salmon. She sank quietly like a seal beneath the gray green of the still surface, pulling down my underwear while rolling into my arms. My feet lifted from the bottom while I pulled her into my saline grasp. Water filled my ears, my mouth, I was drowning in passionate gasps of seawater. I sought her lips, alive as fish. Her mouth laughing bubbles. I pushed against the sea bottom with my feet, carrying her back up onto the beach where I wrapped my coat around her cold, shivering body.

As I was wrapping my coat around her, I glanced up into the field. It was at that moment I first noticed the grand mountain of roses close by the forest. The green twisted tangled red rose mound was alive with bees and humming birds.

Between the mountainous pile of roses and the forest was an old orchard with apples, ripe, simple, hanging from trees that hadn't been pruned in a long, long time. Some of the trees had fallen over, with new young trees sprouting from the older mother tree tops where they fell to the surface of the meadow.

A golden hued deer, along with her dappled fawn, were eating yellow green apples, partly concealed by the thick, high field grass beneath the apple tree. Now and then they stood on their back hooves, reaching high for apples still pendulously hanging from the tree. Crows stood, grasping top branches, bending over at the apples hanging beneath them, feasting. We watched them pecking and poking at the ripe apples, tearing out ragged white chunks. They were flinging a rain of shredded apple chunks down onto the thick orchard grass among drifts of ancient yellow daffodils.

The briny salt air hushed, the incoming tide rose higher, rocks that were at first visible as small islands in the cove submerged, disappearing from view. The sun set lower.

The ducks returned on the dampish hushed air, gliding over us while sliding to a stop, landing on the surface of the mirror like cove. The blue heron, this giant pterodactyl-like bird, its long neck extended, flew in a long gliding motion along the backside of the cove, finally settling on the end of the large floating log out in the cove. Coasting to a stop while lifting its large wings, it settled, with its customary harsh loud cry, on the end of the log. It stood there a moment adjusting its wings, and then stood stock still, becoming one of natures many natural sculptures. The cormorant, which had been drying its wings on the same log, flew. Other large, grunting, croaking flocks of cormorants flew in from around a near point, settling in high, dead cedars, leaning out over the quiet water.

Crows flew over our meadow in large noisy flocks, calling back and forth to each other while flying back somewhere into the deep virgin forest.

Cats paws of ground fog started obscuring the bottom of the orchard. Small field depressions here, then there, filled up with fog like ivory meringues in a jade bowl of grass.

Firs and cedars held at the tips of their

branches droplets of water, suspended and hanging like bejeweled earrings, lit by the slanting early evening sunset. In every dangling droplet was a miniature reflection of the sky in the top hemisphere, while the meadow and cove were reflected in the bottom hemisphere. The world, in that small cove and old farm, inhaled. All was stilled by the coming night.

We continued watching as small fingers of light grey diaphanous sea fog seeped off the surface of the cove, sliding into small creeks and depressions along the shore, eventually reaching the forest, while sliding up and sideways across the fields.

Small islands and rocks, the far shore all were visible, then not, then visible again as the late afternoon sun lit the cove. Sable brush strokes of trees with birds and branches hung, dangling golden, green, silent. The misty cool fog filled in behind the barn, then just as quickly fled.

In the upper field behind the mound of roses stood the sagging barn with twisted paths worn into the fields. They lead to and away from the barn like a compass rose. The barn, we could see, was large. It had a moss-covered, cedar shake roof. Pigeons of various forest colors were strutting and preening on the peak, while iridescent green barn swallows flew in and out through the crazily sagging doors.

Hints of marine red lead paint and white trim were here and there on the doors and window trim. The siding was pierced with open, glassless, staring windows. There were gray hand-split cedar boards going from the ground to the eve.

Little white field mushrooms were everywhere along the paths. Some were in fairy rings out in the middle of the fields. Some fairy rings had depressions in the middle of them as though something had been buried there. Hans and Annette walked up to the barn, as Juliet and I stood outside our car putting on warm, dry clothes.

Helping her into her coat I held her for a moment from behind again. I lifted up her luxuriant red hair from her neck, then, hesitating a moment, kissed her there.

She turned in in my arms facing me murmuring, "I love you." I thought in the memory of that moment that there were no answers, no questions, simply that I was there, that I kissed her, that she was there and responded. Showing up is vitality.

Vital is that reflective seminal moment, the upward breaking of the earth with the first green spring shoots of a daffodil, now that is a story told.

The fog drifting in out of the cove cleared a bit. Diffuse filtered broken sunlight lit trees to golden green. The upper ends of the field lay couched in lengthening late afternoon shadow. We kissed again, then walked up to the crazily slanting barn in one of the old cow paths worn deep into the rich green pasture.

As we got closer to the barn, we could see that it was close to falling in on itself. Some of the posts were surrounded with small scree slopes of finely chewed sawdust. These chewed posts were torqued and buckling in places. When the beams and roof rot in the rainy Pacific Northwest, the rest of the building soon follows. As long as the roof holds out the rains, most wooden buildings in the rain-damp Northwest survive.

This beautiful old barn was losing its battle with persistent nature and gravity, a lethal combination for a wooden building. Though the graceful roof, now moss-covered, the crazy slanted doors, and the roof perforations all made for a beautifully decorated ruin.

The doorways, all of them, were no longer straight. The barn was slanted in the direction of the winds. It needed crutches, none were available. The barn's undulations over the soil looked like some slow drunken glacial dance. Looking through the circus-like slanted barn door, the stalls, with rusty stanchions, were hanging quietly, waiting for cows that would never come again.

Over the closest stall, on a beam, was a small, square, green can of mint salve. The loft was visible through a square hole in the ceiling above the stalls. Through hole in the roof I could see a patchwork of blue sky with rapidly drifting clouds.

Late soft pumpkin yellow sun lit the dried, manure-covered wooden floors, while the hand carved beams were lit up. As our eyes adjusted to the dark interior, we could see that it had long since been used as a barn, and was used instead as a place of storage.

I followed Juliet through the door. I

spied what looked like a monkey skull protruding out of the dried manure. Kneeling down, digging it out, I found that it was a doll's head, porcelain and antique. A shiny face in well composted manure. The little doll's head was in perfect shape, nestled and protected by the dried, rotted manure. The cherubic face with its glowing pink cheeks, dark hair, its blank face with clear blue fixed, staring eyes, was startling. I gave the head to Juliet, she put it her pocket. Some where a dog barked.

I walked another few feet, hitting my head on a chandelier hanging from the ceiling. It was bronze, with cast unicorns and Scottish thistles. Mice were running along the rafters at our approach. Pigeons, cooing nervously, flew back and forth in the gloom, with their anxious sounding flapping wings.

Annette called to us to come and look at what she had found. She pointed down into a wooden trunk with a rusty lock. Opening it, she discovered old books, magazines, photo albums, a black feather boa, as well as doll dresses and other moldering papers and handmade baby cloths.

We all gathered around as Annette pulled out of the trunk an old, worn, black paged photo album. It had a moth-eaten green velvet cover. Opening it, we looked at faces from another time. The photos had been taped by their corners to the old black pages. On the first page were faces of people from a time long ago. Formal people in formal dress, men with glistening dark hair pulled straight back. They wore white shirts with high, old-fashioned collars, and dark black suit jackets. They all stood stone still, staring into the lens of the camera. There was one man who was looking off to his left, as thought out there somewhere was his future.

One young man, whose face is now lost

to history, moved when the shutter was re-
leased. He goes into eternity as a blur.

The women, with flowing skirts and white shirts with sailor-like ties, all peered into the camera from an age now long gone.

They were beautiful, these people from long ago. They stared bravely with courage into that soundless grave yard, where nothing ever explodes into smiles or laughter.

Where were they going, crawling from infant childhood, brand new, down the face of time? Was that a fragile scream from someone, from one of them? They couldn't crawl far, not in seventy years.

As I looked at their eyes, I thought of my own eyes this morning, while looking at Juliet's eyes.

"Someone will remember us," I say, "even in another time."

On one page a couple in some kind of formal Scandinavian outfit stared solemnly back at us. I looked into their eyes, could they look into mine? I think not.

"There is nothing more dangerous to us than age."

The Scandinavian woman was blond, pretty, with her hair parted in the middle. She wore a dark full length silk dress, which was tightly fitted at the waist, with small white pearl buttons all the way down her front. Her elaborate braids were fastened with little pink and blue crinoline ribbons, like small elaborate candies.

The man had dark hair, parted in the middle like the woman's. He had ringlets, a handle-bar mustache, a full beard. He wore a white suit coat with gold military epaulets, and a white vest with a gold watch chain. At his side hung a gold-handled sword in a blue scabbard. He looked frankly and sincerely without fear into the lens and his future. Could I be that brave? I thought.

On the next page small twin blond blue-eyed boys, each a mirror of the other in sailor suits, stood with their arms around a large long-haired black dog. The dog was harnessed to a small two-wheeled cart with an older man with a raggedy, bushy mustache and pointed beard. He wore a foreign cap with a bill, and stood nearby the boys and cart, holding the collar of the dog.

As Annette continued to turn the pages, time changed. There were pictures of the same couple on board a ship with teenage sons. Soon, on the following page, there were pictures of oxen pulling logs through deep, dense forests. There were forested skid roads where men were riding on logs holding reins, while being pulled by huge, swelling, dapple brown draft horses.

In other photographs women were standing on top of huge fallen trees, dressed in men's trousers. They were smiling. Men, leaning against those same huge fallen logs, were holding long shiny whip saws, their eyes looking directly into the camera from long ago.

The men looked serious. Some were smoking pipes, while others held smoldering cigars clenched in their teeth, which protruded through their full beards, smoke drifted from their cigars.

The photographer is a pickpocket. How could these couples, these people, staring with innocence, ever guess the guile of the photographer behind his one-sided glassy lens. The photographer who would, and did, carry them beyond their deaths.

That he could, and did, carry them beyond the orchard, the virgin forest, their first love, their last love.

The photographer silently conveyed them. He carried them, lighter than photo paper, through the ages. He dipped them into chemicals as they drifted out onto the cosmos. Smooth as wet bones slipping down the white cosmetic tubs of time, looping, gliding, sailing along into and ultimately out into infinity.

I remembered a time in Italy, when a grizzled old peasant threatened me with a long knife. I had tried to take a picture of his donkey, loaded with loaves of bread. My Italian friend told me the old man was fearful I would steal the soul of his burrow.

Turning the next page in the old album there were pictures of war carnage, canons, young men, farm boys who I am sure had other intended futures beside war. They were marching in lines with eagerness to kill someone, anyone, just get it done, get the war over, get home to the blond girl across the country road, on the high plains of North Dakota.

To burn buildings, grenade young European men with similar ambitions to their own in life. Kill these young French boys, slaughter the youths of Germany. Meanwhile these boys from Europe were equally as eager to get back to their farms in Normandy, their families in Mannheim.

Who sets this horror in motion, who sent them to grind and gnash others, who, in another kinder, gentler time, would be their best friends?

Marching off the Euro-bound transports, some madly hoping to rape women, their first, shoot point-blank the French parents, salt the earth, kill their French cattle, piss on their soil.

They marched, singing, "We are going to kill the Kaiser," defiling off ships at small docks, off loading military supplies.

These young men in olive green wool uniforms paraded in front of buildings with French names. Preening young officers sitting astride beautiful horses, saluting with one finger at the camera.

Many who stood staring into the lens would never see the green green grass of home. They would be slipped into the sod, maimed, destroyed, a skull cap bullet ridden, a face ravaged by a German 88 mm, dried blood. Blood shouldn't be dry, should it? In a healthy twenty year old, what changed? I will tell you, the wailing siren call of war for young men, death be damned. I will be there, I am 18 years old, I will never die, I can't be killed, until a sniper. In another photo three soldiers smiling, happy, handsome, were in front of a military field meal cart with mud caked wheels. Each one held a ladle, except one who held a rifle pointed at the camera. We assume he didn't pull the trigger.

They were in a muddy, smashed down field of corn, the corn crop was destroyed. Around them were men with aluminum plates; in the far background a dead horse, its legs up in the air.

The handsome young man looked familiar, perhaps like one of the young teenage boys on the ship.

On the next page was pinned a WWI

purple heart. Annette took this, pinned it to her purple satin chemise, laughed, told a story of her heart being bruised, then she sang a little song about her bleeding heart. We all laughed. Was it funny? Not really, millions died, we knew this, but of course uneasily laughed anyway. Life is this way sometimes.

Another photograph showed pictures on the top deck of the Eiffel tower. Young men stood in a semicircle on the top deck, with beautiful dark young French women. They were crowded together in the anachronistic lens of the eternal camera. Like the long bow that is the camera, be joyful in your bending, for your image will fly where you cannot.

Each young soldier held a bottle of French champagne. Standing in front was the same man that had pointed the rifle at the camera on the previous page.

He was kissing, in an intensely sensuous way, a strikingly magnificent heavily tattooed dark young woman. We can see the outline of his hand inside her white silk blouse, her breast is cradled in his hand. Her nipple shows between his ring finger and his middle finger.

On his ring finger is a golden band. If we could see the inscription on the inside of the ring it would read "Hal loves-", but we can't read it because it is inside the gloriously beautiful French woman's blouse. A tattooed red heart shows on her throat in the open V of her white blouse. Her face showed desire with her graceful head tilted back, inviting his mustached lips. His face shows, just for the lens, heat.

The next page showed a clearing in a virgin forest of gigantic fallen trees. Virgin trees were fallen on top of each other like pick up sticks. The gigantic virgin trees were burning, sparks and smoke shooting into the sodden rainy grey skies. People standing stone still near the burning logs were posing for the camera. A blurry black and white dog was walking toward the camera, maybe the same dog that was pulling the children's toy wagon.

The last page in the album held documents from the US Army Culinary Corps, saying that Harold Sorenson had been honorably discharged from further duty on the last day of May, 1918.

Tickets on a transatlantic ship, New Atlántico, bound for Le Havre, France, were stapled to the page, no return ticket. The page also showed a photograph of a log cabin in a newly cleared field, surrounded in deep forest by a newly planted orchard. In front of a barn a young man, smiling, looking into the lens, stood holding a small calf. The calf was looking at the camera as well.

By the young man's side, a very pretty blond woman was holding a red rose. There was a small amount of blood on her finger, from a thorn? She was looking at the camera, and we all thought, Were is she now? I was struck with a sense of time, a sense of love for her, a sense of understanding, not understanding.

In the photos the people were lost and discovered. Lost to time and discovered by us. Were we next in the breech? We now knew we were standing in the very same barn as the one in the photograph. At the bottom of the box, wrapped in colored paper, was another small box. When Annette opened it, we found more pictures that were chewed by the teeth of time, damaged beyond recognition, by mice, moisture, rot, book worms, gravity.

If the only thing you leave in this life, I thought, is a photograph, luck's a chance. A rat born on a different day from you can take away your identifiable, recognized image, masticating.

Quietly, insistently, the rat chewing here, then there, until your existence on your only photograph is like the dash on your tombstone between your birthdate and death date; it is a mere nothing. After all, the dash on your tombstone isn't your life experiences. It is only an abstract meaningless marker, signifying nothing. What about your first love, learning to ride a bicycle, kissing someone, your first steps, your first coupling? The dash says zero.

Some photographs, stuck together and ripped, tore when we tried to part them, the faces gone, the arm gone, the gorgeous spring day, so magic, gone by the glue.

There were partial pictures of the blond woman lovingly holding a child in her bare arms. One arm, part of the babies head, chewed off by mice. The child, what was left in the ruined photograph, was wrapped in a blue embroidered blanket. Behind them in what was left of the photo was a cabin with small roses planted on split cedar arbors.

Another blurry dog, this one all white, was stopped in mid motion, again walking toward the camera. What is it about dogs that they can never stand still for a photograph?

Next were photographs of a little boy sitting on a blanket in the sun. Another photo showed a small grave with a white gravestone, with a carved white marble dove on top. On the stone was carved "Baby Sorenson." I thought of the "S" carved on the sign at the end of the driveway. A small, beaded necklace lay at the very bottom of the box, and fell into pieces in her hands when Juliet tried to lift it out.

Scattered throughout the rest of the barn stacked here, there, were kerosene lamps hanging from rusty nails driven into beams. Rotting jackets hung on similar nails, rusty old bedsprings, jars, tools, boxes, all in some sort of decay. It looked like a tragedy where the owners simply walked out. Perhaps they ran, stumbling, maybe fearfully falling one dark, rainy night in that old recognizable confusion called disheveled despair. They left, they ran they fled, they died; what ever the reason, they never came back.

A rusty old Majestic stove was slowly collapsing in on itself. It was under a hole in the ceiling where rain fell. There was no one to protect this, this whole rotting collection of someone's very sad life.

Precious objects have no defense.

On the boxes, where the roof had let in years of rain, boxes, trunks, suitcases, all had split, cracked, fallen open. They revealed more moldering cloths, a moth-digested feather boa, rotting shoes, a ceramic cup from the New Atlántico, unrecognizable, destroyed bits and fragments of someone's grim, unhappy life.

All of a sudden, the dark, scary, forbidding coldness in the barn made us all turn at the same moment to walk back outside. It started to rain at the very moment we walked to the barn door. A dark heavy purple blue tattered cloud passed over at that moment. We were at once entranced yet frightened, uneasy.

There hung in the air in that barn the feeling of ceaseless sorrow without end. Something about all of these belongings, abandoned, made a mystery in the eternal void of time. A void in time where we were now standing. In this moment we felt our blood coursing, felt our hearts pounding, the vitality of our youth yet, yet, heavily the feeling of other's doom.

At the moment we turned to walk out of the barn, drops of water started to leak through the broken shakes. We watched as the insistent rain began once again dripping its continuing, ever so gradual destruction of the old stove, the moldering, musty baby cloths. The dripping rain continually, drop by drop, was destroying precious, unrecognizable history. This is the day we have.

For what ever reason I thought of my mother reading to me:

"What day is it?" asked Pooh.
"It is today," squeaked Piglet.
"My favorite day," said Pooh.

As we looked through the crazily slanted barn door, the rain shower hammered harder. While we stood there the shower, just as suddenly as though someone had turned off heavens spigot, passed on down into the lush green meadow, out into the cove.

The meadow now seemed like a burial, beneath the verdant sod were skeletons, rising to greet the night. Cows and horses, cats and dogs, babies and what?

Next the evening sun showed beneath a long low grey rain cloud. A faded misty rainbow painted dully over the sun landed far out in the cove. We didn't see a pot of gold.

As the cloud passed, the evening sun came out even farther from behind the dark cloud, its Jesus rays slanting lower, raking across the sunken fields down near the beach. In the waning light, the rolling grass, plants bedecked with glistening drops of rain water, all became be-jeweled magic.

As we stood looking out through the

arch of the old doorway, the large pink pile of roses was in the center. In every arch, in every void, there is unexplored mystery to discover. Mystery exists in the void. The somber dark green forest set the backdrop for the mystery of this gigantic pile of pink and red roses.

As we stood waiting for the last large vertical drops of rain to stop, we all exclaimed at once. For in the middle of the large pile of roses, protruding from the top, stood the remnants of a gray beach stone chimney. Entwined with vines, thorns, and roses, there, protruding through the tangle, barely visible, were bronze crossed swords, now these many years later, patinated to mint green. We walked out of the barn while a few large raindrops continued to fall straight down.

Juliet said what we were all thinking. "This is the cottage in the photographs in the old trunk in the barn."

We all remembered the photos, small roses, now giants, planted on little spindly cedar stakes, now completely covering the cottage. The young faces, now the rose covered cottage, the young, fresh cedar barn, now aged while bit by bit collapsing. The fields, now bigger and deserted, had no cows, no joyous running children, no people, only time distant memories. There were the old barn, the chicken coops, the monstrous pile of roses with the cottage tucked inside, all a reflection of what once was, and would never be again.

"We are our memory, we are that chimerical museum of shifting shapes, that pile of broken mirrors."

Life intrudes, death concludes.

As we approached the covered cottage, we could find no way in. Finally, peering into the tangle, we saw a porch post standing on a large beach rock. The rock was still covered in jagged snow-white barnacles.

I don't know what I thought except that in this tangle of roses lay another new mystery. What the mystery was I couldn't know. I did know that as we all clawed and fought our way into that pile of thorns and fragrant roses, we were excited, apprehensive, and filled with curious expectations.

Fear fills the bowls, nourishes procreative energies, and like the dying fir tree, produces a prodigious crop of cones for new generations.

We finally found the porch. It was a covered porch, and, like the whole cottage, a tangle of roses and vines. The porch was sagging where one porch post had washed away. Stepping on vines, crushing roses, we finally reached the door. The door painted a musty, powdery blue, was closed but unlocked. The door opened as though someone had walked out that morning. We stepped into a small kitchen, noticing a hand-pump at a white sink. Over the sink were two windows, still intact.

Through cracks around the windows where the cottage had settled, blossoming roses had found their way in. They were blooming inside, sort of a green house, giving the kitchen that ambrosial spicy fragrance of rose. The small kitchen table was still set, places for two, while faded, embroidered sagging towels still hung by the sink. On the back of the door a black and red checked wool jacket hung waiting for its now dead, long-gone owner. The threads where the jacket was hung were strained. The cottage, as we all spread out looking this way and that, appeared to be like an antique venerable old tomb, completely undisturbed. The undisturbed smell of so many decades was one redolent with rose, pine and stale air. It seemed as though the cottage was simply waiting, had been waiting for a long time for the owners who never came back.

Hans went looking for wood for the old fireplace, which was still sound, as was the rest of the cabin. A surprise, considering the look of the place from the outside. It appeared that the entire cottage was held together, in reality supported by the grand tangle of pink, sweet smelling roses. The cottage was dry inside, power dry. There were mouse dropping on the counters, spider webs in the windows, ageless dust on the floors, but dry, the roof held.

Juliet prowled around looking at books, paintings, pottery, and the old finely made violin colored construction of the old growth fir.

Over the beach stone fireplace mantel, glued to the wall was a mahogany

colored mat of woven cattail reeds. On the mat was a geometric painting in red and black of a hawk, northwest coast Indian style.

The wind dropped with the sunset.

A loon, with its high sharp ovulating song, called out in the cove. Each of us momentarily stopped whatever it was we were doing, listening to this messenger calling to us from nature. The call echoed deep into the beach and drift. The call, natural as a clam, sharp as early morning sun rays, filled the cottage, the cove, and as quickly faded. Its reverberations and echoes continued down the bay until dying away in the damp evening air.

Annette climbed a ladder that went to a loft over part of the living room. She shouted down that she had found the bedroom. The bed was still made, though the quilts, she said, were destroyed by rodents and the biggest of rats, squirrels.

As the room continued to darken, Juliet found on the mantel two antique kerosene lamps. I could imagine that they had only recently been blown out, except the kerosene had dried, little by little, in dendritic patterns years ago. Even a moth, seeking light at some indistinguishable time in the dead lamp, twisted its dusty wings somehow into the lamp, and found only a prolonged death trap with no way out.

On the floor beside the fireplace, Juliet found a sealed can of old kerosene. She twisted open the sealed cap and, miracles of miracles, found liquid kerosene. She filled the lamps.

Striking a match on the stone fireplace, in the ever-darkening room I saw her face momentarily in the yellow sulfurous glow of the match. She was beautiful. Her red hair long and wild from our plunge in the icy salt water. Her face, classical, with chrome red eyebrows over deeply sunken glacially blue eyes, resembled sculpted stone. I see her like that for only a moment in the flare of the match. She then turned, lifting the cut glass chimney off the lamp, lighting the cotton wick, and next, the room, which was warm, dark, black, was awash in sunset yellow lamplight that filled the room with the scent of burning lamp wick and ancient kerosene.

The fireplace burning as well filled the room with the fragrance of burning beach wood. It gave each of our faces a summery, pale yellow glow.

As our eyes became adjusted to the dim light, we saw there were shelves of books, some chewed on by mice. There were candles bent over in a horseshoe shape, small tables, old rockers, one small window pane broken out, beneath it on the floor was the skeleton of a long dead pigeon. Beneath the broken window the unremitting rains, eternal since 1917, had rotted the floor.

Setting near the old beach stone fireplace was a wooden box with an aged Indian rattle, painted and finely carved in the shape of a bird. The carved bird had a long orange ivory bill. It was covered in light dust, laying on dried kelp on top of the cedar box, which I now saw was of bent wood with red corners. The top of the box had a geometric design. Near the box were also more stacks of books, and magazines partly covered with a moth-eaten red fox skin.

Unbeknownst to Juliet, we had all stopped what we were doing, watching her as she lifted the red cornered box to a small upright blue painted wooden barrel setting near the fireplace. Painted on the barrel was a roman numeral "X" in glossy yellow.

She picked up the ivory billed rattle, shook it in a round-about rolling sound. Its hoarse sound was reminiscent of distant rain on leaves in the forest. The rattle inspired respect, and the desire in me to chant ancient dirges.

Laying aside the magazines and fur, she lifted off the thinly carved painted lid. She reached her hand into the top of the box, pulling out a white beaded bag. Next, looking under where the beaded bag had lain, she gave a small cry turning to us. It was, she discovered, filled with loose handwritten pages.

Some were poems, written with purple ink on parchment paper, old and fragile as onion skin.

There were letters, some still in their envelopes. Some envelopes had stamps from France. There were sheaves of paper clipped together, resembling handwritten short stories. Interspersed with the writings were sketches in pen and ink. Lifting a random sheet of yellow parchment from the box, Juliet held it up to the lamp in the darkening cottage, and with soft and reverent voice began to read.

Chapter 3
September 1917

September 1917

Once again Harold I am writing to you hoping you get this sexy letter in your foxhole. What else can I offer you from this great distance, but my thoughts on paper? The offering of my eager body, since you are not here, and I am not there, I can only give to you on this simple paper. Be assured, Hal, if you were here I would ravage you. I know this since without you I am only left with my own body to ravage.

Well anyway, my sexy note:

Close your eyes, think of my lips, Harold, my red lips. The insides are soft moist pinks with my glistening saliva, picture this Harold. Your sweetness enfolds me, warming me, I get butterflies. They flutter and flit through my whole body. I'm walking naked. Can you feel the cool breeze from the cove tonight, my feet cool on our fir floors, our rose cottage floors? I can, it's late summer now. Closing my eyes I feel your soft moist breath on my ear, was that a caress?

Wearing no cloths, I stood on the wet orchard grass this evening in the rain. It was raining hard, I stood there just for you. Picture this, the rain falls straight down, causing dust when it hits the dry summer ground. Even though you are not here, you are, since I can feel your enthusiasm sweeping through me. At first the rain was cool, huge droplets of rain, then later, steady rain. My wild blond hair looked like it was painted on my head.

The rain water ran down my forehead into my blue eyes, over my lips, your lips, Hal, into my willing mouth, finally down and under my chin, following my throat, then flowing around my naked breasts standing like river stones in a creek. My nipples became erect with late summer tickling rain, water trickling, gliding around them. The rain, insistent, as it always is, found its way down the rolling whiteness of my belly, your belly. I held my arms outstretched like Jesus on the cross. Finally, and Harold, I could really feel this, the rain finally reached my, your, rose red delta forest between my dripping thighs. Finally at the bottom of the red forest, water slowly dripped from wisps of my red pubic hairs. I could feel it, Harold, and it made me shudder. It was almost like your tongue.

I am way too sensitive these days.

When drying myself off with a towel I become heated down there, you know what I mean, Harold. I never want to say too much about us personally. I never know who is going to read your letters. Foxholes, from the little I know, are small and crowed.

I am filling the house these days with red roses, tea roses, yellow roses, as I watch the vermillion metal sunrise rising over the black hills in the distance, the sky robin's egg blue.

Harold, let's carefully and seriously look at this, plain and simply I am drifting insane without you. You are not here, I am alone. My insane drifting isn't all drifting, more like a race to the bottom of my ability to hang on.

All I have in my aloneness are my own

poems, and the very few notes from you. Very few, Harold, will you ever write? God!

At times sitting by the heat of the fireplace I can still taste our first gentle intoxications of love, musty red wine on my rouge lips. You, with your rich dense beard, tickling me. Passion, that was our beginning, where tonight it lightly rests on my quivering imagination, hot breath. Remembrances of your passion sustains me, most of the time.

As I stood in our loft by our bed this morning, looking out the window to the sunlit orchard and our new barn, I discovered new virtuosity in my hands, my thoughts, as my palms and fingers passed over and into my own body, with you nestled warmly in my mind.

I lay back on the duvet, closed my eyes, dreamed, shuddered, remembering when.

There was your violin music, my heart plays your music. I pulled the bow across your violin today. It squawked, I laughed.

My dark, rich blood purls through me, engorging me at your thought. You can see here I am somewhat maddened at the thought of you and my lack of love, write!

How did you arrive in my soul on the wings of a rainbow, or was it a raven? Did you whisper something to me, or was it your look? Did you dare so much or did I?

Was it written on the lifeline of your palm? Was there music? Love changes everything. In a sunlit silken tent, the roar must be the sea.

Chapter 4
1980

As she finished reading, Juliet looked up into the loft and waited for the tears in her eyes to go away. We all were unsettled. All of a sudden what had been a lark, finding the old deserted farm, then the barn, with its decaying mildewed objects, the rusted old Majestic wood stove collapsing in on itself, how many meals for whom and when?

We could almost hear, "Hal flapjacks and eggs are ready. I fed little Harold already, come on in before it gets cold."

"Coming," calls a voice from a young man holding a small calf out by the barn. Are the reverberations of his call still traveling like the duck's wake on the still waters of the cove, so small but still, minutely rolling forever? Eternity? Zero to infinity.

Then when we broke into the cottage, it all took on the persona of these real people, real just like us. Were we guided by a credo from someone from the now distant pass. Were we simply barbarians at the gate? Breaking through the gates of a place where we had no right to be?

We were being transformed by meeting someone that had lived, then died, many, many years ago. How did this person die? How many ways are there to die? We, in some strange fashion, were trying to greet and shake hands across time with those long gone.

What about the future, will someone reach back in one hundred years to shake my hand?

And what of the dash through life between births and deaths?

To time, does time even exist? Death is not even the so-called blink of an eye. To be dead for a second is the same as being dead for eternity, to become a part of the eternal celestial heavens forever.

Spinning on axial trajectories with the only hope that in perhaps fifty thousand years, give or take, our finely ground heavenly dust will return to the spot where we were born. What are the chances? Minimal.

Will the "old home town still be the same when I step down" from the clouds? Will our Mama and Papa be there to greet us? And down the road will there still be my dear sweet "Mary, hair of gold and lips like cherries"?

But of course, by then someone will have taken our place. We are talking fifty-thousand years after all. Or will we stand somewhere on the same cloud, looking back, and what once was, will it never be again?

Time has little to no meaning. We scoff at the life of a fruit fly.

"What is recalled by faded flowers?"

Juliet took a poem from the box and read:

In silence

Secrets drop

Heart to heart

Only lace apart

A sweet rose scent from eroded memory

A place where a rain drop fell

Perhaps beside a shallow brook

Where blood touched my wing

In this summer garden

Sinking in delight

My passion is you

Night transforms my naked body on upright legs

Rain drenched dark

Rain drenched day

Thrust, I lie still, I part

I sink in joy, rise to minstrels

Radiant firmament above

Moss below

The roar must be the sea.

"The meeting of two personalities Is like the mixing of two chemical substances. If there is reaction, both are transformed forever."

Next Juliet pulled a tattered sheet of paper from the box, and with it a torn piece of fragile yellow newspaper that was clipped to it. The lead article was this:

"The assassination of Austrian Archduke Franz Ferdinand on 28, June 1914, will surly lead to a broader world war"

Juliet read aloud the article. Then, laying it aside, she looked back down into the box and gasped. "Hans, come quickly," she said.

There, lying like a venomous snake, at the very bottom of the cedar box under where the 1914 newspaper article had been, was a partially exposed pistol handle. It was wrapped in a shrunken blue baby's sweater.

Carefully lifting it out, Hans discovered a .357 magnum hand gun, with pearl handles. Scattered randomly under the .357, like a nest of copper snake eggs, were handfuls of .357 hollow points.

Chapter 5
1914

Hal, when I read this article once again, this death of this Archduke, I thought how the war, this thing, this muddy endless ghastly vile brutish war, rages everywhere.

The history of man-kind is the history of war. Why kill? Where is there safety? Who are these men that started this slaughter? Hal, how can men, warm hearted men,

Christian men, family men, cross the world with the sole intent of massacring their fellow men? I'm becoming sick of heart and mind. Don't they have farms, families, parents, wives, loved ones, babies, and future plans?

Where are you tonight, my love? Black clouds roil the stygian night sky, the moon sails partially occluded, heavy rain and wind dominate my side of this world. Even our little cove is storm tossed. This night, this threatening night, is dark, so dark I can't see you even in my mind. It is too black to think.

Stick with me on this thought, Harold, these thoughts of you only are all that buoys me up these days, so as I said, stick with me on this.

I am recalling that one day, you know the one, of course you must, I will never forget it. You stood me in the forest with my back against a tall mossy tree. You were laughing, your face wet from warm rain. You looked like the bad little boy I know you can be.

I remember your lips finding my throat and my open collar, then your fingers on my blouse buttons, then the clips on the back of my pink embroidered bra, then, finally freed, my breasts rose up, seeking your moist lips, licking tongue. Surely you haven't forgotten.

In the deep forest there is moss, essence of earth, smells of growing gardens, potatoes, maybe a carrot. There is also a small creek. In its gravelly, pebbled, sun dappled bed, alongside an old water-logged cedar, where the water gently eddies, I am waiting for you to return from the sea, Hal, stick with me here.

Shadowed by maples, watched by ravens, I am your female salmon, waiting, moving my frayed tail softly, just for you. I am silver sided in places, though gashed by my journey from the sea, I am still bright silver in places. Centuries of my kind have guided me to this exact spot, in this exact stream.

I shudder, I shake, spawn flows out into the stream, this distant creek pulled me through alder pools the color of tea. Here in this dappled quiet I sense a mother's primal rage ripping apart my ravaged and torn body. A bubbling screaming beneath the surface draws me on distant magnetic energies, about which I know nothing.

I only respond from my green depths to my queen, Aurora Borealis, to my other queen of the night, my moon.

I dream, salmon dreams of lovers as I see you force your way up the rapids. I wait. With your milt and my spawn I willingly die. I am waiting, please don't let me die alone.

Hal, I feel your mouth close on my ear, your tongue across my lips. My hands will themselves, I make no apologies.

How long had we known each other? My hands always will themselves when I am near you.

Remember that summer night when we lay aside the soft moss by Uncle's trail, under the tall firs by the Indian grave? My eyes couldn't adjust to the dark, only my lips and hands. Thinking of you I sup at the well of longing, finding in your pure, spring-fed depths purling waters, nourishment.

Your eyes, your eyes? They were over me, under me, around me. My shadow, like a night owl in flight, flowing in candle light, undulating on your manly belly, like the shadow, a hawk gliding over summer fields. "I heard the owl call my name tonight."

Tonight, sitting here, the firs and cedars dripping heavily, rain falling, sometimes so hard I can't hear myself think, only a slate grey roar, I'm tired of this life.

The river may make the salmon stronger, but this salmon is ready to die.

Dear Harold, I don't know the riverine valleys of our love by name. I know them by your scent, returning king salmon sensing home.

Holding you while you hold me, I am lost and discovered. Remember how you would say in bed, "Assume the position," then you would roll over and I would spoon around your manly body, my leg over yours. When my arms are around you my senses fill with perfume in the crescent of your strong, elegant neck.

You are my world. I know this: you will seek my stream, even from France, you will swim the oceans, turn from the sea into my riverine mouth, drive and thrust against currents and furious white water rapids.

Look for me, Hal, when you thrust your powerful tail, shooting that final rapid.

There, as you silently glide into quiet waters, you will find me in a tessellated pebble bed in sunlit shallows. You will find me Harold. I will be waiting, only for you. Together at last, the deep Pacific will only be a distant pelagic memory.

Do you remember before you left, we had a drought? I do. I remember the firs were all sun burned yellow on the west side. The creek went dry and we had a bumper apple crop. Remember all the applesauce. Everyone had apples, I couldn't give them away. Ha.

Life seemed so simple then, so easily lived, straight forward and timeless.

Pump a bit of water at the sink into the kettle, place it on the hot, shiny old Majestic. Easy as that, pull some carrots, dig a few potatoes, grab some onions, take the head, feathers, and guts from a chicken, make a broth, salt and pepper, and a bit of lovage, put on the lid. Really Hal, was life ever really that simple? All that, those time-separated days, now seem like a dream in someone else's dream. My summers have turned to winters, my crops have withered and died. Me? I am starving, dying, from lack of your nourishment.

For the last two weeks, it has been raining steadily, and if that were not bad enough, I can't be near you.

Since you left, I am lonely. I must see you, yet I can't. You are near in my thoughts, yet so far away. Today, I worked in the cottage while watching the heavy rain falling outside the windows, drumming thickly on the roof.

I thought of the time in our little tent in the forest when we first met, remember? You let me hold you like a child while I could hear the insistent raindrops falling on the tent roof. I was nearly breathless at your nearness, so tenderly exciting, our infant love.

Your breathing was soft and even, warm, moist.

Do you remember that day I rubbed lotion into the palms of your hands? Your eyes were closed, you were smiling sweetly, I wished that the moment would never end. That is what it is always like when I am with you, I wish the moments will never end.

When you part my thighs, I think of the next moment when I shall again part, then again, and again. Is that what love is?

That time when we walked through the forest, past the Indian grave to the lake on your birthday, we started out in the winter sun, hugging, laughing, then there was that little, light mist. Mist was landing on your eyebrows, on the fine blond hairs of your mustache. First it was so sweet, so soft, that we weren't prepared for the mist turning to light rain, then rain, then heavy rain. What fun that was, you looked as though every airy thing on your body was pasted to you by the rain. I could not have loved you more than at that moment. If not that moment, then maybe it was at the cottage later. Oh, I don't know, I love you madly all the time. I'm losing it, Harold.

Anyway, I am sure you recall, that day you filled our old collapsible WWI rubber military field tub in the middle of the living room in front of the beach stone fireplace with hot sudsy water. Remember, you gathered it in buckets pouring off of the roof outside, heated it on top of the red-hot great polished Majestic. You warmed the towels in the warming ovens. Oh God, I fell in love, think hot scented cotton towels, maybe at that moment. Yes, I think it was then I fell forever even more in love. No one ever did anything like that for me, imagine little me.

Rainwater pouring off the roof is so soft, the color of tea. When you pulled my sopping wet clothes off you said it was like skinning a deer. You laughed, saying

I looked like a frightened fawn, naked as I stood before you in the heated yellow firelight. My body, wet, glistening in front of the flaming fireplace, my breasts steaming, my whole body steaming.

I am lost and discovered in my thoughts of you.

You are not here tonight, yet even now I feel, as then, when your rain-wet lips sought mine. We walked back through the woods, you with both of your strong arms around me. Do you know that when a goose loses its mate it dies? Not trying to be funny Hal, but your hen is slowly, well not so slowly, dying.

Remember, I know I say remember a lot, but what do I have but memories, of one who once told me they loved me.

"Everything remembered is dear, endearing, touching, precious. At least the past is safe, though we didn't know it at the time."

That day so long ago, we walked, mouth to mouth, rain runneling down our joined faces in salty sheets. Me, aroused at the restlessness of your clothing, and frightened at the fragility of our love. I still am.

I need you tonight, my need is helped by sitting here in our bed, up in our fragrant warm cedar loft. While looking down at the snapping fire in the fireplace, writing, I remember you lifting me from the bath that night, and as you held me close, you told me my fragrance was of our herb garden, one of rosemary and thyme, ginger and rose. While I luxuriated in the bath, you drifted fresh rose pedals over me. They floated in little pink islands, so fragrant. In our loft that night we lay together on top of the feather duvet. It is always so warm up there when the fireplace is going.

As I lay close and secure the world outside our cottage was a maelstrom. The winds thrashed the huckleberry salal cedar forest. Rain, always rain, ceaselessly pounded on our shake roof. Branches flew, trees lost their tops, cones, like small grenades, rained down.

As I lay that night beside you, I remember feeling wonderful, so secure, so sure that my world was safe in your presence. I felt at anchor, in protected shelter in a world that was now at war.

Maybe I should have realized that the lightning flashes were really guns and bombs reflected from the other side of the world.

I recall that night so clearly because it was then, just then, when I was most at peace, that you told me you were going away.

"Where," I remember saying with a broken voice?

"France," you said. When I started to cry, I could also see tears in your eyes.

It was then that you asked me to lie on

top of you, to be your blanket so that we would never forget that night, or be cold in a bleak, frigid world.

I am thinking of that moment as I write this, because instead of lying on top of you, I sat astride your slender thighs, settling down with you deep inside me.

"Leave me with child," I cried.

You, my great lusty man, crying into my palms, said, "Get ready."

Oh, Hal, I was never so ready, the vibrations of your thrusting rhythms reached my tingling toes, what magic.

The rain, wind, raw grey flashes of lighting, our tears, the heat of the loft, war, ships at sea, nerve gas, where are you tonight? I am no longer at anchor, or at peace, I am storm tossed, adrift, with no oars.

Harold, I somehow know you are at last coming home today. You will probably think I am unbalanced. Why, I am convinced you are homeward bound, I don't know I just am. Well, the truth is I dreamed it last night, that's how. I know at last that you are coming to me.

I am waiting by my window to catch a first glimpse of you. You will be smiling, your blue eyes will be glistening from the mist this afternoon. I will feel, for I know myself, I will feel breathless.

I am already excited.

Hard, cold rain will be falling on you while threading your way through the slanting rain. Great winter drops will be falling on your heated face. I am sorry to tell you that last, but today, like most days it seems, it is raining. I'm sorry it has to rain on the day that you are coming home. Really Harold, I can see it all. It is you!

After all, you will have walked a long way to see me. I'm looking sometimes down toward the cove, even though I know you couldn't come that way, because of the stream and the old logging bridge being washed out.

Here is my plan when you arrive: I will kiss your lips, press your wet face against mine, give you sweet Turkish coffee, warm your hands by cupping my breasts, they miss you too.

I know this, you aren't here yet, but I know it still, I know you are coming.

You love me!

Hiking through Uncle's trail, threading the dripping deep forest, I wonder can you see my red candles burning? If you look you'll see me through my rain drenched window, with candles, at my table writing. What do I write? Well today I wrote: There is a place in me tuned on gut strings, stretched taut by love. Many days now I feel like those taut gut strings are going to snap.

You see Hal, waiting seems so long, too long.

What is it the Spanish say? "Life is short, but the night is long." Life is short, and the nights are nearly unbearable.

Wait, is that you I see weaving through the trees? In your high black boots or, oh no, I just went to the door, hoping, praying, but guess what? It was only last years bracken fern waving in the wind. Not yet, you aren't coming yet. It is only my own eagerness playing little jokes with me. I knew you wouldn't come this soon, but maybe later this evening.

Maybe you won't come. After all, it is starting to blow harder now. A large limb just hit the roof, along with the near constant pelting of fir cones. Rain is hammering sideways against the windows. What do the Indians say? "One must never go into the forest when it is blowing hard."

I can see falling water dancing in the cove when, occasionally, the last of the evening sun, like a brilliant gash in an angry nightmare, shares its tortuous yellow beam.

It is then only then that I can see falling

rain dancing, creating circles on the cove, dropping out of dull pewter skies onto dark mustard water. The ducks are all bunched up out in the middle of the cove behind the big rock.

You will come, won't you? You are coming, you told me you would, didn't you? You are as eager as I am, aren't you? The candles are burning lower, they lick and flicker, little wavering red tongues of heat. As I watch them, hot and molten, a little tear of red wax is breaking over the rim of one drooping red candle. Slowly, ever so slowly, hot wax runs red down the shaft.

I am looking again, for the hundredth time, at the place where the trail breaks from the forest onto the field, hoping to see you. I shouldn't tell you this, but watching the candle's tears, my own tears are also making their way down my molten flushed cheeks.

Oh God, please Harold come to me,

come.

Well its morning now, and I decided to just get drunk again, God damn it, Harold, when you say you are coming you need to come. I'm not eating breakfast these days, coffee upsets my stomach, Four Roses calms it down.

Walking the old trail to the beach today, I looked at last year's dead leaves on the trail, looked at the broken thrashed branches, I saw storm-tossed trees, broken, bent, fractured.

I foolishly jump in terror, especially when I am drinking, as huckleberry branches seem to reach out to grab me. Salal branches wave in the wind, they are monsters of darkness. Hal, the damp plastered leaves, so crushed, remind me of last year's love, do you still love me?

I am always cold without you, with you I'm heated. Fir roots are after me, small bugs crawl, gnarly, twisted roots poke out of the earth. I think, sorry to say this, that someday soon I will be buried there, that I am and going to die. I quake at the thought, without you, Hal, to hold my hand.

Did you ever notice the pond where the heavy rain pools over the trail when almost to the beach? The one with the massive logs across the bent creek? Where there is that distorted cedar growing through that enormous huge rotted spruce? Where last year's leaves lie on the bottom of the pond, all dead? Those leaves are me, Harold, all dead, outside and inside. Without you, I am a fungus, bound to the side of a tree, no life, just existing. I am a mushroom, smashed in the roots, alone. I am a dripping sodden mess without you.

Have you ever noticed how dying things all look the same when reduced to a skeleton? Somewhere I read that all starving people, when they die, all look the same. They are reduced to skeletons, and all look

the same. When the skeleton decompos-
es into dust and mud, we are all the same,
Hal, yet all different. As I got to the beach,
the tide was high, a raven was calling from
deep in the forest, I could hear an answer-
ing call from out on the point. I am calling
to you, Harold, answer me, please. But then
you never do, do you?

Why then, Harold, did I wake this
morning, my heart a rain-drenched window pane, my mind a whirling weather-
vane, longing at least to hear your name?
I will tell you why I feel this way, because
you didn't come the other day, Harold,
that's why.

Rest, I tried to sleep, but was too excited. When you didn't come, I thought how
could it be? How dark, cold, lonely I feel.
Upon lifting the corners of my dreams this
morning, I saw myself where I was once
more, once again, a lonely little girl. Beautiful, pure, sweet, soft, I saw myself weeping,

separated by great distance from myself.

Some days, longing, I cry like a baby. I put my head on my folded arms on our little writing table, I close my eyes, sob. My stomach hurts, my mind won't work right, my mind works wrong.

All I have is this sharp, though veiled, acute longing.

It is the place of women, whose men are at war, to never know if they will return or not. You could be dead for a month and I would never know. Ghastly.

I seek in the folds of my thoughts my remembrances of your face, your ever so ap-pealing eyes, but what I delight in is finding your inner person. I am always thinking of you. This I shouldn't tell you, but I can't re-ally remember what your voice sounds like.

Today I went for a long walk in the woods on the old trail to Uncle's little tar paper shack. I looked at the early morning sun slanting through the trees, lighting up one side while the other side was in dark. The bark was filled with silver yellow white lichens. As I stood for that moment, lost in thought of our many walks, I remembered the night that Uncle brought you home in the wheelbarrow, when you broke your ankle. How you said, lying in the wheelbarrow, looking up at the sky, you said small alder leaves were falling, easing the pulsing, throbbing pain of your broken ankle. Grandpa puffing a Lucky Strike as he wheeled you along.

As I stood today looking at the trees, I remembered how you used to stand me against the trees in that sunlight, kissing me, looking straight into my eyes while your busy loving hands were unbuttoning my jeans, then rolling down my panties.

It all seems so simple now, so natural, yet so very golden and opulent. Life is funny that way. Small happinesses of the moment have a way of becoming golden upon looking back.

One of the most hurtful circumstances about sorrow is the way it invites the crowding in of memories, of happier times for comparison with one's present misery.

The picket fence around the old Indian grave is still standing, though someone has stolen the Chilkat Indian blanket that was over the old canoe. Pieces of the blanket are still nailed to the canoe where they tore it off. One corner fragment was a woven raven riding on top of a killer whale, the loose strands where it was ripped from the main blanket flutter in the breeze. Even though Uncle has been gone from us for many years, I could still hear his anvil as I walked slowly along, lost in thought. The ring of his hammer on the anvil was his signature, I remember you saying.

It is strange how the ringing of a bell can clear the air and one's thoughts as well. Small birds sing duets to each other. I wish

I could trill now, that you would hear me and trill back. I do so love you.

Do church bells still ring in the battle fields? I read in the paper the other day that the Scots marched into Verdun playing the bagpipes. I recall that you use to play "Over the Sea to Skye" on your violin, but now, music along with joy, has vanished from my life.

Where do you sleep at night at the front, is it ever quiet? It is so quiet here at night that I can hear the beat of my own heart. It distresses me. I roll from left to right to sleeping on my back to still my hammering heart.

Are you always frightened? I am for you, your safety, and hope-pray that you will one day return to my arms. Old Mrs. Woolfolk said to me the other morning, "Our men folk go off to war, and we live and die each day in dread. It is our lot as women."

It seems like a dream this lovely summer day to think that there were times when you were near that I didn't even kiss you. Isn't that funny, we of course can't be together all of the time, but then when you are away that is all I want. So here, Hal, is the question: If I am not loved physically, you are gone, long gone far away, can I continue to love you fully, emotionally? I try, I yearn, I lean in, but in the end it is only me and the horrid mirror. My reflection is not yours.

I am working our garden everyday. Our old neighbor brought me glass topped canning jars, which I hope to fill for winter. The lettuce greens are up as well as the peas. Calendula is everywhere, and at night the nicotiana perfumes the garden. Violets are everywhere in small fragrant clusters. I am sorry this letter sounds like I have no life without you, I have. However, life without you is never like life with you.

I am plainspoken. You used to say you liked that about me, do you still? We all change, but tonight, for what ever reason, I am drunk. Maybe that's it, whenever I feel like I can walk, my head up, my speech sort of clear, that I am somebody.

Please try to understand, but somedays I walk around saying, "I am nothing."

Relationships are based on mutual support. With you gone, every day, every night I seem to be always trying to pick myself up, starting all over again. I'm getting tired, so weary.

Tonight, I am going down to the old dock to see if the perch are running. Last week there was no paper or mail because of some war time strike, so maybe today. Did you receive the mittens and socks? The wool is from Claude and Mindy. Uncle sheared them up in the field by the barn.

Good night, my love. I am wearing your blue silk Russian shirt to bed tonight, nothing else. I try to imagine your feet down at the bottom of the bed with mine. P.S. I love you!

Saturday morning, sunny, warm. I walked up the driveway this morning and the mail came. I was out for my walk anyway. What a surprise.

Hearoldson, our mail man, came just as I reached our sign that you made at the top of the drive way.

He pulled a perfumed purple letter out of his old leather pouch. He smiled broadly and said, "Looks like a letter from Harold," winked at me, then gave me your letter. "We thank him for his service Mrs. Sorenson." He is a kind old man. He also gave me another pint of Four Roses whiskey, winked, and said it might help me sleep better. He said he takes it at night with a teaspoon of honey and a little lemon, if he has it. He perhaps forgot that he has given me Four Roses before, which I drink, no lemon, no honey, some nights straight out of the bottles.

I clutched your perfumed purple parchment letter to my breast, running down the driveway, grinning like some imp. As I ran, I looked over my shoulder, shouting back at Hearoldson, "Thank you, thank you!"

I stopped, and sat on the bench you made, holding the letter to the sun. I saw your letter silhouetted inside, thinking at last a letter from you came.

I greedily ripped it open, happily, giddy, even laughing, and what on earth, this earth? What the hell do you mean?

Was this letter for someone else?

Harold, what, WHAT! Do you mean? I can't even find words! How can you write this? Who is this in the photograph? Am I supposed to know her, care a piss-ant for her, give a damn about her? Her, her, oh God, Harold how could you?

Last night I slept on the porch after writing you the above. I couldn't sleep in our marriage bed, how could I? Am I supposed to believe what you sent, that note, that nothing? Then, Hal, then, that shitty tattooed woman, her picture? Harold, do you realize what picture you sent to me? The French tart up on the Eiffel tower, her head back, waiting to be kissed, you, Harold, grinning your bad boy stupid smile. God, I detest you right now.

Harold, it's me! I know that look, remember, I know you, or used to.

Remember old Grandma Woolfolk, the chicken lady? She once told me that in the spring the young roosters get a wild, crazed look in their yellow eyes, then try to mount every hen they can catch. They pecked the back of the hen's combs until they bleed. She said the only way to get their attention, to make them stop that action, was to hit them in the face with a flat board, or put them into a stew pot with lots of broth and vegetables.

You look like this, Harold, a stupid cock with a rooster's dumb boy leer. You are a cougar, aren't you? A real rooster, aren't you, with your cock-a-doodle squawk? Have I really, really ever understood you? I am beginning to wonder, and I don't like it, none of it, the French tart least of all. You are a bastard, Harold, a real pig's ass. Me, the fool, moping all over the farm, my tears salting the meadows, my shouted grieving echoing off the forest, drunk and stumbling.

Where I seek closeness, you revel in French thighs and distance. The mine fields aren't in France. I am the dumb bell. Who is this spectral, this ghost dancing around me? My soul is shrinking.

I no longer see a way for me between you two, except to be quiet, to listen, and hope sometime, someday, you will come to clarity.

Never get caught waiting, my father once said. Why am I waiting? Why in the name of hell am I waiting, while you kiss her deeper than I want to know, finger her, and more?

That cheap necklace, acrid French perfume, French candy, a negligee, all in that box you sent. Was the negligee hers? Your hand was on her bare breast, I could see it through her sheer white blouse, then this?

I remember, about an hour before the postman came today, thinking my breasts were your first, that I was the only one, that I was your first. Now?

What a deranged fool I have become. Will you never come home then?

I know you love me. You can't live over there. You don't even know the language. She is not as pretty as me, you are such a nitwit, why do you like her so much? And her tattoos, what respectable woman does that? If you were home, well for instance, remember how much fun we used to have up at the lake? I bet I am more fun.

You are soft shit, Harold. I thought that sudden ghastly death was everywhere. Where are you? Where the hell are you?

Clearly the Eiffel tower is not on the gas-filled field of war. Where are you, then, that death is only the little waving pink clitoral death on top of red French sheets?

When I close my eyes, bombs explode, rockets fly, smoke, insidious mustard gas, shrapnel, rubber suits for protection, horses die by the thousands. All is chaos, blasting destruction, life and limb at risk every second.

Oh, how do I know, how can I know what life in flooded trenches, bombs bursting, men bleeding to death in the mud? I am not there, so how could I know what war is?

I have some ideas though, I at least know this much:

Bayonets, sharp and killing, of course, 8 mm mausers, without a doubt, German

88's, yes, red silk sheets, no, bombed out French farm houses, yes parted thighs, no, black pubic bushes, no, pretty dark girls, no, dead peasant parents, yes, bloated cattle, yes.

You can see here I am confused. Love them all, just come home to me. I am at the mouth of your river.

It is dark now. The perch are running, I am distracted. I am so distracted that I fell off the porch this morning. I went through the Four Roses that the post man gave me, what seems so long ago now, in one night. Did you know you can buy Four Roses in gallon bottles?

Emma died last week, we buried her up in the field in one of the fairy rings, I forgot to tell you. She was healthy, with her new calf one moment, dead the next, her calf, adorable tan creature, died beside her also. The vet was perplexed, and wouldn't charge us for the visit.

I felt funny today, wondering what, well, maybe if I died, what if I was buried in the field up in the fairy rings on the sunny side of the big rock? Up there where we buried Coco and Emma. Do you bury bodies where you stand, fight, and die?

You see, I can't think like you. All I see are the four square walls of our cottage, and the side of old Rose as I reach under her for her milk. I sit at the little three-legged stool, milk her like you did. Her herbal breath is somehow reassuring. I take the green mint salve can from up on the spiderwebbed beam in the barn, pull off the square top, plunging my fingers into the iridescent jelly. Scoop some salve, rub her teats, and her soft white grand roseate bag of rich cream. I massage her utters, plus massaging my own hands at the same time. It feels sensual, especially with you long gone.

Rose always turns her head, smiling at me when I rub salve into her breasts and massage her. Even as I rub her, her teats ooze milk. I am not a cow, but I liked it when you rubbed me. When you suckled me, I didn't feel like you were a baby. I felt we were the same person, we were one, mouth to mouth, inhaling each other's breath.

I dreamed on the smoothness of your wet lips, your tongue on my nipples, do you lick hers, the tart? What did you say once, that you could see the flush of red emotion passing over my face as you stroked me? Does her dark French face flush? At times these days with my depressing loneliness I rub Rose's green mint jelly salve on myself, shameless I know. For God's sake, don't let anyone read this Harold.

I lay back in the fragrant hay in the barn and pretend that my hands are your hands. I am not embarrassed.

Today when I got up there was a small redheaded bird dead in front of the kitchen door. The dogs sniffed it, Kleocatra, sweet kitty, merely walked around it. I think maybe it flew into the window since I saw small red feathers, glued by blood to the window.

Do you ever think of me? I only ask because of the letter, the tattooed tart, my fractured, shattered trust, and fading belief. They say the war will be over soon, will you come home then? I will never marry again. I am screaming out loud into our very empty cabin, shouting it even though I am writing it.

I will never marry anyone but you. I have in my hand tonight your purple heart, it also came with the letter. For valiant service above and beyond the call of duty. What does that mean? I mean, I get the gist, but what have you really done to receive this? What is a French purse? The note said you alone took a French purse with 7 Krauts. What does that mean? Sauerkraut?

I took the pin on the purple heart and poked a pretty little bleeding heart of pin

pricks on my forearm. Then I rubbed char-
coal dust from the fireplace into the little
wounds. Now I am always reminded of
you since it doesn't wash away. Not that
that matters much since I don't bath often
anymore, too much trouble.

Do you remember the red-cornered box
from Piupiu-maksmaks, filled with hops
that you made beer with? I dumped out the
hops, and am now filling it with your letters
and my ramblings. It feels reassuring to me
to have all of your letters in the same place.
I read, reread your letters at night, look at
your photographs, thinking how strong
and proud looking you are. In the photo by
our bed you look so soft, very lovely. Say
you are coming home, tell me something,
not just this soul shrinking eternal silence!
Desiccation.

Some days I am sure that I am dying,
that I can't go on living. My heart pounds,
my head aches, the tips of my fingers go

numb, I fail at the simplest things.

I can't light the stove or fireplace, so I am always cold in the damp. I can't seem to wash the few dishes, I forget to feed Kleo, I forget, and so do nothing. I don't eat or drink, except for whiskey, that seems to help. I shouldn't tell you this, but the other night after drinking way too much, I tacked your picture up on the wall and threw darts at it.

Some days I want to hate you, but then I love you, then I hate you. Today I don't see you, I see the French tart. So today is easy, I detest you.

Why in the hell, Harold, did you send me her picture, and those stupid perfume impregnated nothings of gifts? Send nothing, just come home. I am losing weight, I think I look better, but even my bras are getting loose.

I walked over the path across the ridge to the sea again. Today, like most, is disorienting and frighteningly lonely. Today all is gray, the color of reeking long dead.

The sky is dark, roiling, swirling into its self with even more blackness. It has been raining all day, just spitting, as the saying goes. All is muted, calm in the cove, while icy damp wind, causes whitecaps out in the channel. The trees creak, cry, whistle, moan, up on the ridge, as they rub against each other from the strong gusts high up in their crowns.

They bend far over in the gusts, then slowly straighten back up when the gust passes. Every now and then one of the late leaves lets go from a tree, glides, spins, stalls on its way to the forests floor. The ground is soaked, so trees are falling all over the place from the wind. The heavy continuous rains are over flowing our creek, it is running out and right over the grass, across the fields, down into the cove. Flowers are bent, beaten by rain to the earth, with dirty yellow faces. As I looked into the mirror this morning, I saw dead flowers.

I received your last nothing note, do you expect me to say I am reassured? I am lonelier still, why must you say things that you know will hurt me?

My answer? You know my answer. I refuse, even more, I won't go on living without you.

But maybe that's what you want, for me just to go disappear in a hole in the forest, so you can live here with your French tart.

I am sorry. No, damn it, I'm not sorry. I shouldn't have said that, but when one is drowning in dreaded sadness, what else but confusion and self-deprecation?

I thought to myself the other night, what schemes will they try to get rid of me so they, you and your tart, can move in? You see, Harold, with so few letters from you, and no hope, I quite naturally can only think the worst.

Walking up to the barn in blackness to-night, don't ask why I was walking in the dark, just quirky me being drunk again and adrift, I felt I could smell your fragrance. I closed my eyes, walking in blackness, following the scent.

I read where, in your war, there is the stench of dead animals, dead humans, rotting food, and anxious sweat. Does she smell, the tart?

Well anyway, my story, I will tell you what, even though I wasn't going to tell you since I knew you would scold me. So this, I fell, tripping on an old apple branch. It was all so wonderfully innocent. I had my eyes closed, walking in the dark, drifting on your smell, and bingo bango, I was on my face. Four Roses, sure, I admit it, had a part.

I have just returned from seeing old Doc Davis. Guess what, I broke my right wrist. I heard it break, though it is not displaced, Doc still put a cast on it. I couldn't tell if it was the wrist or the dried branch that made the snap. Have you ever had a cast? It itches like mad. The pain is deep in the fracture. Whiskey helps.

Tonight, evil rain, cursed, damn rain, yet it comes constantly, again with high tree-toppling, tree-cracking winds. I don't want to worry you, war and all, but the rain running off the roof has washed away a support post under the porch. That side of the porch, on the meadow side, now sags a little.

My candle that I had left burning for you snuffed out. I left it by my bedside window, the wild wind pushed open the window violently, frightening my flickering flame to death, that is, it blew it out. It blew over the glass candle stick as well, no harm done though, it didn't break. The wind blew so hard that it blew the blankets off my feet, scaring the hell out of me.

I jumped up, slipping on the rain-wet

floor. Don't you worry about little ole me. I'm ok, just a bump where I hit my head on the bed post. I know why I fell. I think I had three or four shots, I forget, of Four Roses before I went to bed to help me sleep, so falling, it didn't hurt too much when I slammed my head. I seem to need to drink more just to get to sleep these days.

Getting back to my feet, I stumbled over to the open window. Reaching out to close the window, I looked out at the cove. The full moon, yellow, muddied by grey, rapidly scudding clouds, lit the surreal maelstrom of racing white caps. Each high wave carried a little bit of the moon on its shoulder. Behind the black hills, in the near distance, were sheets of lightening. I, of course, thought of bombs and war. I couldn't sleep after that, so I took several more shots of my new best friend, Four Roses, finally passing out when the sun started to come up.

You can read as well as I, Hal. When I read that last paragraph I wondered if I am going "around the bend" as Grandpa Levenseller use to say, or you know, going nuts. But then I think crazy, insane, ruined, no, I think it's simply longing, just lonely longing. I am weary.

Each day bending like a sapling in a strong gale, I am being bent closer and closer to the loamy earth, which I am beginning to welcome with open arms. Dust to dust, you know? Ha ha ha.

Today I put broken whiskey bottles in the garden to kill the horrid green slugs. I used to put salt on them, but as they were expiring during their slimy death journey, they left white trails of their dying over our grass. All I could think of when I saw that was their rasping death, and then yours.

Drinking Four Roses, now my drink of choice, I have plenty of empty bottles to break up.

Drinking makes me forget. Don't you worry your little self, you bastard, I can still climb the ladder to the lonely loft, or LL as I call it. Ha Ha.

Although, having said this, I did break your favorite cranberry colored drinking glass on the stone fireplace the other night, I am sorry, I am sorry, I am sorry I'm alive.

I read this again this morning. Mornings are harder, I am sober. But still it's about the slugs, or the weather, the dead cow, the dead bird on the porch, my aching wrist, our dead baby, or you know, don't you, it's you.

I love you.

This late afternoon just after my fifth shot, when I was feeling pretty good, an old man, unshaven, came out of the trail from the main road. I hate to be interrupted when I am drinking.

He had wet blubbery lips, he was bent and slouchy, hobo like. His faded wool shirt was black and green check, you know the type, his loose, dirty looking paints were held up by logger's suspenders.

He asked me about the cows, the Indian grave house, then, in a kind of sinister way, all the while peering over my shoulder, trying to look into the house, asked if my mister was around. I just silently looked at him. Then he took a step closer and asked did I maybe have a shot of whiskey for him? He chuckled, his front teeth were rotted. When he laughed he coughed a phlegmy, gaging cough, then spit out this grey splat on the ground by my feet.

I pulled my Danish knife on him, and told him to run while he had the chance, because there would be no second chances. I would kill him if he didn't run. He ran, boy did he run, like he had seen the proverbial ghost. I'm tired of men these days, the more I drink, the more tired of them I get.

I poisoned mice in the barn again tonight. I tasted a little bit of the poison on the tip of my finger, it burns.

The mice and rats have been chewing little Harold's baby clothes that we put in the cow stall after Lulu Belle died. There is a leak in the roof just over Lulu's stall so now, damn it, his cloths are damp from the weather and starting to mold.

I took Harold's little blue sweater the other day and washed it in scalding hot water, thinking to kill the mold and get rid of the mice piss smell. Well what do you think? It shrunk to a little blue wad. I seem so confused these days. I know better, but did it anyway.

When baby Harold died I just could not give him up. Who can separate from one's infant's warm moist pink suckling lips? My nipples still become erect when I think back to those times. Why couldn't I bury him, why did I carry him through the house, out into the forest for days. I'll tell you why, really very simple. I so wanted him to be alive, even though he was board stiff and started to smell, I still believed he might be alive.

Only until we wrapped his little knitted blanket around him, and placed him in the hole in the ground up under the apple tree, did I know, how horrible, that he was gone.

Is there a God?

I go up to his grave every day, and leave treats for him, apples, carrots from the garden, once in a while a piece of toast.

These little gifts are always gone the next day. When little Harold, Oh, I can't say it. Anyway, he was so warm, so cuddly, God I am so alone, distracted, so maddened, so miserable.

Tell me something. Write, why don't you write? Every day when Hearoldson, I should tell you I am getting tired of him too, when he comes, nothing ever from you. Hearoldson never brings me any relief.

When he comes by, there is never a letter from you, nothing, nothing. NOTHING.

Hal, you are my sole slippery path to sanity.

I dug out your pearl handled .357 pistol again this morning when I was looking for a scarf in your drawer. I have been kind of lazy the past few days.

It is damp, yet I haven't lit either the stove or the fireplace. To hell with it, I drink. I put on your sweaters, two at a time to keep warm. Anyway, in with the .357 there was a box of what the label said were, "hollow points." I picked one up, it was cold. I could feel eternity ending in that small copper chamber of death. It had a hole in its lead rounded point, sort of like your penis.

I can't believe I just wrote that, please I beg you, don't show this letter to any of your buddies.

Anyway, I took the .357 out to the living room along with a pocket full of hollow points.

I took five slugs, as you used to call them, filling five chambers of the .357, leaving one empty. Then, just for the hell of it, I laid the pistol on the kitchen table. I sat down with a shot of Four Roses, and like we use to do in school, I played spin the bottle, only this time with the semi-loaded .357, and not for kisses.

Don't ask why I did this, I know it is double action, you told me what that means, so I pulled back the hammer and saw the magazine rotate one turn.

I spun the flat .357, on the table, it's cold blue metallic surface reflecting sunlight coming in the window, the pearl handles flashing at each rotation of the pistol.

Guess what? I spun it, and it turned and turned, then slowed its turning, until finally it came to a stop with its barrel pointed right at my right breast. Wow, who could guess?

I looked at its menacing presence lay-ing there on the table, pointing its deathly barrel right at my chest. Don't ask, but I pulled off your two old blue Scottish sweat-ers, which I was wearing, then reached be-hind my back, and undid my red bra, the one you use to like. I did that so that if the pistol went off it wouldn't ruin your/my bra. As I said, it was pointed right at my right breast. I touched my breast with my index finger exactly where the bullet would have entered.

I reached out, spun the pistol around so that it was pointing away from me. I pick it up by its white pearl handle.

I lifted it up, and aimed it at our wed-ding picture, sitting where it always sits on the fireplace mantel. My hand was shaking so much I couldn't fix it, because I was aim-ing it right between your eyes, a small tar-get from across the living room. I switched the pistol to my left hand, picked up my unfinished shot of whiskey and downed it. I switched the .357 to my right hand, aiming it right between your eyes again. My hands didn't shake this time, I lined up the front and rear site on the bridge of your nose, pulled the trigger, and guess what? Click!

Luck's a chance!

I took the pistol with some slugs out to the porch, looking for something else to shoot, and spotted a slug oozing its slimy way across the wooden porch railing. I aimed, pulled the trigger, shooting the hell out of the slug. Guts every where, slug dead, railing destroyed, end of story. I'm sorry, but I hate slugs.

Later, taking the FR bottle, I went down to the cove, the wind blowing harder. One thing I will tell you right now, again, I forgot to take your ear plugs, my ears are still ringing. It's hard to hear much when my ears ring like that. That pistol weighs a ton, especially holding it up with my slowly healing right wrist.

Walking down the beach the tide was high, there was very little beach exposed. I shot a fishing cork that was floating by, missed it, of course. Shot four times, and missed all four times. But what power, what kick.

I walked on. You would never guess or hope to see something so hideous and pink as this in a thousand years. A near coral colored sea lion had washed up on the beach, it was all dribbling and bloated. Little pussy rivers of putrefaction were running into the sand by its gigantic decaying body. I could see small white maggots where its rot exposed its insides.

I couldn't stand down wind, the stench was assaulting. It has been there for some time. Something about its smugness, its invincibility, its whiskered mustache, its immovability, all of it, especially that mustache, all of its stink and conceit, reminded me of you not coming the other night like I know you said you were. One more thing about your mustache, it reminded me of you kissing the tart.

Trying to move you was like trying to move that reeking monster. I indulged myself by walking around that malodorous, gassing lump of deadness.

Finally I shot it in its pus-filled head, right between your/its dead, staring eyes. Some of the pus that exploded from the blasted, bloated head landed on my face. What a loathsome, sickening stench. I emptied the .357 five more times into its bloated guts. Then I reloaded, shooting six more hollow points into it ghastly face. I finally succeeding in blowing its snotty nose off, exposing its worm filled brain. I walked on, feeling better than I have in a long time.

Three more shots of Four Roses, no pain, at least for the moment.

You know what? I started to laugh.

Was something funny? I couldn't stop, then I started to sob. Was something sad? I laughed, cried, laughed, cried, sat on a log, pointed the .357 at a crab in the sand between my feet, and pulled the trigger. Guess what? No crab. I walked on.

I shot a dead grebe on the beach, it was missing a foot, probably drowned, maybe in a fisherman's net. Each time I shot the grebe it jumped about a foot, that .357 has death written all over it.

I took one of the grebe's metallic green feathers and put it in my, or rather your, hat, in the beaded head band.

I'm sorry I said that about you and the sea lion, but you did promise me you were coming home the other night, I'm pretty sure. That sea lion, for some reason, set me off. I saw you. It's stupid whiskers, it's puffed up, swollen, arrogant face, with its blank, unresponsive eyes.

When I go off I disappear to myself, I

become someone or something else. Who am I without you? I don't know any more.

Anyway, I go off.

The other day I started screaming, Kleo ran out the door, and hid under the porch. I ran out the door as well, into the deep forest behind the barn. I didn't look nor care where I ran, I just kept crashing through the blackberry bushes, the thorny devils club until I ran head first into a mossy old maple, falling at its foot, bawling. My arms and face were gashed, I totally lost it, Hal!

I go off, more and more, almost all day every day now. I try, well that's a lie, I don't try to control it, because I can't. Four Roses doesn't help like it used to.

Surly somehow, somewhere in my rampaging mind, I knew you couldn't last being in France with all the beautiful French girls. Death of all kinds all around you, surrounded, I mean, well, you sent me that tattooed French tart's picture too.

Anyway, like I said, when I go off in that stark staring moment, I know for certain I can't claw back, and that you will never come back. That paralyzing moment somehow becomes a moment of clarity for me.

Even without Four Roses, in that moment of crystal clarity, I know for certain, I shudder to even say this, I really know, I without a doubt know, you will never come back to me.

I am a simple country woman, Hal, however I can and do read.

Did I hope, even after seeing the photograph of the French tart, then reading those poison letters? Oh my God, yes, I must admit it, I hoped endlessly.

"Oh, if only you were faithful to me."

You see, my hope for you never flickered, never wavered, but I read what you sent, the letters, they contained so little for me to continue living.

So cruel, heartless, those perfumed purple perfumed parchment letters!

So bruising, so overwhelmingly killing, destroying me, how could you?

That photograph.

You are gone.

And me?

I am dying alone on my own battlefield. My enemy? Myself!

"The fence round her house,
The woman I loved long ago,
Is ravaged and fallen;
Only violets remain
Mingled with spring weeds"

"Fujiwara no Kinsada" 10th Century

To author and artist Douglas Granum, creation is a way of life.

His inspiration is derived from his travels around the world and an appreciation of the unusual — trekking the jungles of New Guinea, enjoying plein aire painting in northern Urals of Russia, drifting down China's Yangtze River, looking at the stars in a Serengeti night sky, and commercial fishing in the storm-tossed Gulf of Alaska.

As an artist Douglas Granum works with and in various mediums including stone, metal, glass, wood, canvas, bronze and of course, writing. From creation in his studio in Southworth, Washington, his paintings, glass pieces, metal and stone sculptures can be found worldwide.

Find out more at DouglasGranum.com

Other stories by Douglas Granum:

JUDITH'S GAP

THE GERMAN MUSIC TEACHER'S COTTAGE

WAR NO PEACE

DEATH AND AFTERLIFE ON EL PASEO

ALONE ON THE YELLOW STONE

OFF A LIGHT

Find out more at DouglasGranum.com